This edition published by Parragon Books Ltd in 2015

Parragon Books Ltd
Chartist House
15–17 Trim Street
Bath BA1 1HA, UK
www.parragon.com

From the movie
DiSNEY
FROZEN

ELSA'S BOOK OF SECRETS

PaRragon

Bath • New York • Cologne • Melbourne • Delhi
Hong Kong • Shenzhen • Singapore • Amsterdam

This book
belongs to

Gabriella

The kingdom of Arendelle was a busy and happy place, nestled high among the mountains of the far north. At night, the colourful Northern Lights often lit up the sky in beautiful patterns.

A kind king and queen ruled Arendelle. Their young daughters, Elsa and Anna, were the joy of their lives. But the royal couple had a secret worry....

    Their eldest daughter, Elsa, had a magical power.
She could create snow and freeze things with just
one touch!

    Anna adored her big sister and the two were
always together. They loved to have fun in the
snowy playgrounds that Elsa created.

One night, while the girls were playing, Elsa accidentally hit Anna with a blast of icy magic.

The king and queen rushed their daughters to the realm of trolls – the trolls were mysterious healers who knew about magic.

A wise old troll explained that Anna could be cured, but he also had a warning about Elsa's power. "There is beauty in it but also great danger," he said. "She must learn to control it."

The troll also changed little Anna's memories so that she wouldn't remember Elsa's power.

Elsa struggled to stay in control of her powers at all times, so the king gave her a pair of gloves to hold them back. She decided that to keep Anna safe, it would be best to stay away from her.

As the years passed, the girls became more and more like strangers. Then, when the two were teenagers, the king and queen were tragically lost in a storm at sea. The sisters felt sadder and more alone than ever.

When Elsa was old enough, she became queen. Guests from far away sailed into Arendelle for the coronation.

Anna was excited to meet so many people – especially a handsome young prince called Hans!

Meanwhile, Elsa was still struggling to hide her powers. She just hoped that she could make it through the day without anybody finding out about them.

To Elsa's relief, the celebration went exactly as planned.

Anna and Prince Hans spent the evening laughing, dancing and talking. They had so much in common! Everything seemed perfect, so they made a big decision....

Anna introduced Hans to Elsa – and announced that they were going to be married.

Elsa was shocked. "You can't marry a man you've just met," she told Anna.

Elsa started to leave the room, but Anna grabbed her hand and accidentally pulled off her sister's glove! An icy blast shot from Elsa's ungloved hand, sending a sheet of ice across the ballroom! Everyone stared in disbelief.

Elsa fled the castle, worried that her secret had finally been revealed and terrified that she might hurt someone.

Everything around Elsa turned to ice as she ran. She stepped onto the fjord and the water froze solid!

Ships at the harbour became locked in the ice as she raced towards the mountains in the distance.

Elsa climbed up into the mountains and with nobody around to worry about, she let all her power loose for the first time. She felt free! A blizzard whirled around her. She even turned her own dress into a beautiful icy gown.

As she neared the top of the mountain, Elsa created a magnificent, shining ice palace. At last she felt like the person she was always meant to be!

Elsa's blizzard had covered Arendelle with snow. Anna knew that she had to find Elsa to thaw out the land – plus, she wanted her big sister back. Now that Elsa's secret was out, they could finally be close again!

Leaving Hans in charge of the kingdom, Anna rode into the mountains. The storm made the journey difficult, though, especially when Anna's horse threw her into the snow. Luckily, she spotted a small building up ahead.

The building was a shop for travellers. Anna rushed
in and immediately gathered up some supplies.

A young man named Kristoff was also collecting winter
supplies. He mentioned that a storm was coming down
from the North Mountain.

Anna began asking questions. If the storm was on the
North Mountain, Elsa would be there, too!

But Kristoff was busy bargaining for supplies.
Feeling crowded, he blurted out, "Now back up, while
I deal with this crook!"

The insulted shopkeeper threw him out of his shop!

Anna found Kristoff in the stable, where he was singing to his beloved reindeer, Sven. She offered to give him the supplies he needed if he took her to find Elsa.

Finally, Kristoff agreed. "We leave at dawn."

"No," said Anna. "We leave right now."

They left in Kristoff's sledge, but a pack of wolves
started to chase them! Anna helped Kristoff to fight off
the wolves and even managed to save his life. Eventually,
Sven was forced to leap across a deep gorge to escape and
the sledge crashed on to the rocks below. Luckily, Anna,
Kristoff and Sven were safe.

The trio continued into the forest on foot. They soon came across a gorgeous winter scene. Anna was more eager than ever to find Elsa – she had to know more about her sister's amazing power!

"I never knew winter could be so ... beautiful," Anna said.

"But it's so white," added a voice. "How about some colour?"

It was a living snowman!

"I'm Olaf," he said, explaining that Elsa had made him.

Anna asked Olaf to lead them to her sister. "We need Elsa to bring back summer."

Olaf grinned. "I've always loved the idea of summer," he said. "The warm sun on my face, getting a gorgeous tan. Just doing whatever snow does in summer."

But Anna and Kristoff were thinking the same thing: summer would not be good for a snowman!

The path up the mountain grew more and more difficult. Luckily, Olaf soon found a stairway made of ice leading straight to Elsa's palace.

"Whoa," exclaimed Anna in awe as they reached the top. The ice palace was amazing!

They approached the front door and Anna knocked. After a moment, the door swung open.

Elsa was worried to see Anna. She wanted to return home with her sister, but she knew that everything would be different now that her secret was out. She also remembered how dangerous her powers could be.

"I think you should go, Anna," Elsa said. "I'm sorry. It has to be this way."

But Anna explained that Arendelle was still frozen. If Elsa stayed away, everyone in the kingdom would freeze.

Elsa admitted to Anna that she didn't know how to
undo her magic, but Anna was sure that they could work
it out together. Elsa knew nobody would ever look at her
in the same way again. But Anna didn't understand.

Elsa's feelings of anger and frustration overwhelmed
her until her powers burst out of her – and struck her
sister in the heart!

Anna refused to leave, feeling certain that she could
still help her sister. But Elsa insisted – and conjured up
a giant snowman to escort Anna outside, along with
Kristoff and Olaf.

As they left the palace, Anna threw a snowball at the giant snowman and he decided to chase them!

The friends ran until they reached the edge of a cliff and then lowered themselves down the side. But the giant snowman grabbed the rope. Anna did the only thing she could think of – she cut the rope!

Luckily, Anna, Kristoff and Olaf landed safely in a soft snowdrift down below. But something was wrong with Anna – her hair was turning white!

"What happened back there? What did she do to you?" Kristoff asked.

When Anna explained that Elsa had struck her with her powers, Kristoff knew just what to do. Night fell as Kristoff led Anna and Olaf to the secret realm of the trolls.

One of the trolls explained that Elsa's magic had struck ice into Anna's heart, which would cause her to freeze solid by tomorrow! But there was still hope.

"An act of true love can thaw a frozen heart," the troll said.

Thinking quickly, Olaf and Kristoff decided to take Anna back home. Surely her true love, Prince Hans, could break the spell with a true love's kiss.

Back in Arendelle, Hans had become worried when Anna's horse had returned without her. So he had gathered volunteers to help him find Anna and capture Elsa.

When Hans's group arrived at the ice palace, Elsa had tried to protect herself. But in the struggle she was hit by falling ice. She was taken back to Arendelle as a prisoner.

Kristoff and Anna had no idea what had happened at Elsa's ice palace. Kristoff took Anna to the castle gates at Arendelle and sadly passed her over to the servants.

The servants built a fire in the library to warm Anna, but she was still getting colder by the minute.

Anna was so glad when Hans arrived. She explained what Elsa's icy blast had done and how his kiss could cure her. "Only an act of true love can save me," she told him.

"Could it be this easy?" Hans asked, his smile turning into a sneer. Then he put out the fire with a jug of water. Hans explained that he had only been pretending to be in love with her so that he could rule Arendelle!

With Anna nearly frozen, Hans saw that his dream was within reach. All he had to do now was to get rid of Elsa.

"You can't," Anna gasped. She collapsed to the floor as the ice spread through her body.

Meanwhile, locked in the castle dungeon, all Elsa could think about was getting away from the kingdom to protect everyone from her powers. She was also worried about Anna – but she didn't know that Anna was back in Arendelle, too.

Elsa became so upset that she lost control of her magic again and froze the dungeon. The ice broke her chains and she escaped!

At that same moment, Olaf helped Anna to get to her feet and come outside. The little snowman had realized that Kristoff loved Anna – and that his kiss could save her!

Anna spotted Kristoff running over to her and she began to move slowly towards him, almost completely frozen. But then she saw something else – Hans was about to strike Elsa with his sword!

With all of her remaining strength, Anna threw herself in front of Elsa. Hans's sword came down just as Anna's body froze to solid ice. With a loud CLANK, the blade shattered.

Elsa wept as she wrapped her arms round her sister. Then something amazing happened. Anna began to thaw!

"Elsa?" she whispered.

"You sacrificed yourself for me?" Elsa asked. Anna nodded weakly.

"An act of true love will thaw a frozen heart," Olaf said.

With her sacrifice, Anna had helped Elsa to see that love was more powerful than fear.

Suddenly, Elsa realized that love was the force that could control her powers. She raised her arms and the ice and snow that covered Arendelle melted away.

With summer restored, the visiting ships sailed away and Arendelle returned to normal.

Anna replaced Kristoff's sledge and his supplies and he thanked her with a kiss!

Elsa created an ice-skating rink in the castle and threw
open the gates of the kingdom – she never planned to
close them again.

Everyone had a wonderful time skating with Queen
Elsa and Princess Anna. The kingdom of Arendelle was
a happy place once more!

From the movie
Disney
FROZEN

All About Me

Add your details and share
your secrets with the
Queen Elsa. She is very
good at keeping secrets!

Name..

Nickname..

Birthday...

Hair colour...

Eye colour...

Address...

Email..

Phone...

Best friend..

Pets...

....

Family...

....

....

My best talent..

My worst habit...

My happiest memory ....

....

Thing I am most proud of..

....

Secret Pictures

Stick photos of yourself on these pages to keep them secretly stashed away. Try to find a snowy picture of yourself to add to the collection.

Stick a photo of yourself here!

Me on holiday.

Me as a baby.

Me at home.

Family Forever

Family is very important to Elsa, especially when she realizes that she has a lot to learn about her sister. Make sure you find out all there is to know about your family and write it down on these pages.

Who makes you laugh the most?...

Who is good at helping you out?..

Who makes the most mess?...

Who gives the best hugs?...

How would your family describe you?.......................................

....

....

....

....

Stick your favourite family
photograph here!

Powers Unleashed

Elsa hides her magical icy powers from the people of her kingdom. If you had secret powers, what would they be? Write about them here.

What would your powers be?............................

....

....

....

....

How would you use them?............................

....

....

....

....

Draw a picture of yourself using your special powers here.

Royal Dreams

Elsa dreams about her life as a queen, and about keeping her powers a secret. What do you dream about? Keep your own secret dream diary.

Date ....

What my dream was about ....

....

....

....

Rating

Date ....

What my dream was about ....

....

....

....

Rating

Date ....

What my dream was about ....

....

....

....

Rating

Date ....

What my dream was about ....

....

....

....

Rating

Rate your dream

☺   for fun

☹   for scary

😆   for fun AND scary!

Perfect Palace

Elsa builds her palace of ice on the North Mountain.
Write about your cool castle here.

Made from..

Number of floors..

Number of rooms..

Biggest room...

Favourite room...

What it's like inside...

....

....

....

What it's like outside..

....

....

....

Draw your royal palace here.

Loyal Friends

Elsa's secret made her feel lonely.
Help Elsa feel a little better by
telling her all about your friends!

Name..

Hair colour...

Eye colour..

Best talent..

What I like most about them...

....

Name..

Hair colour...

Eye colour..

Best talent..

What I like most about them...

....

Name..

Hair colour...

Eye colour..

Best talent..

What I like most about them...

....

Snowy Secrets

What's the biggest secret you've ever shared?

....

....

....

....

What is the funniest secret you've ever kept?

....

....

....

....

Elsa has been keeping a very big secret
from everyone she knows. Are you good
at keeping secrets? Write about them here.

What secret would you
share with Elsa?

....

....

....

....

Have you ever spilled
someone else's secret?

....

....

....

....

Be A Queen!

Elsa was born to be a queen, and she takes her role seriously. Could you be queen for the day? Fill in these pages with your royal ideas!

Queen name..

Name of kingdom...

Name of castle...

Royal pet...

Royal pet name...

List five things that you would do as queen.

1 ....

2 ....

3 ....

4 ....

5 ....

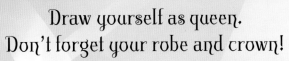

Draw yourself as queen.
Don't forget your robe and crown!

Royal Party Planner

After Elsa was crowned queen, she had a big party to celebrate. Now it's your turn to organize a royal celebration. Use these pages to plan the perfect royal sleepover party.

Guest list:

1 ....
2 ....
3 ....
4 ....
5 ....
6 ....
7 ....
8 ....

Films to watch:

1. ....
2. ....
3. ....
4. ....

Snacks:

1. ....
2. ....
3. ....
4. ....

Games to play:

1. ....
2. ....
3. ....
4. ....